Shopkins™

Once you shop...You can't stop!

D0482795

# THE UPDATED ULTIMATE COLLECTOR'S GUIDE

by Jenne Simon

   SCHOLASTIC INC.

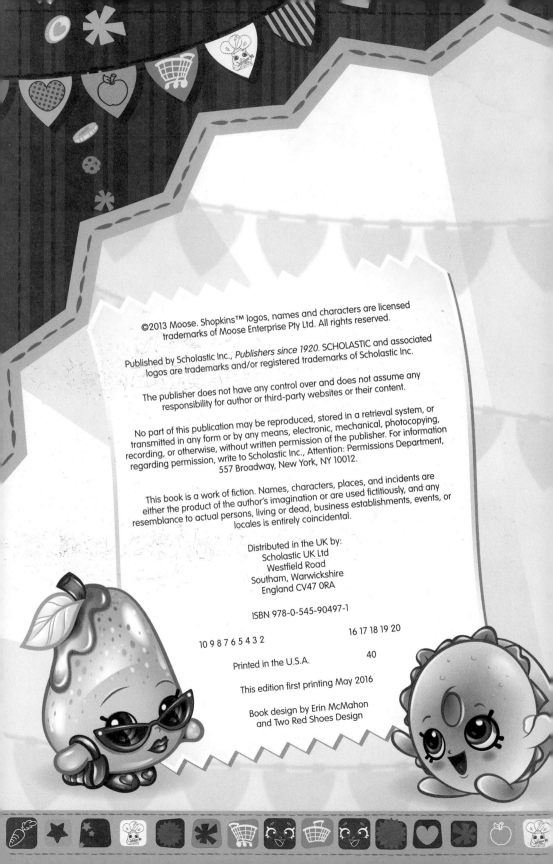

Published by Scholastic Inc., *Publishers since 1920.* SCHOLASTIC and associated logos are trademarks and/or registered trademarks of Scholastic Inc.

The publisher does not have any control over and does not assume any responsibility for author or third-party websites or their content.

This book is a work of fiction. Names, characters, places, and incidents are either the product of the author's imagination or are used fictitiously, and any resemblance to actual persons, living or dead, business establishments, events, or locales is entirely coincidental.

Distributed in the UK by:
Scholastic UK Ltd
Westfield Road
Southam, Warwickshire
England CV47 0RA

ISBN 978-0-545-90497-1

10 9 8 7 6 5 4 3 2          16 17 18 19 20

Printed in the U.S.A.                    40

This edition first printing May 2016

Book design by Erin McMahon
and Two Red Shoes Design

# TABLE OF CONTENTS

**SHOP 'TIL YOU DROP!**

Welcome to Shopville, the home of all your favorite Shopkins™! This updated collector's guide is jam-packed with all the latest characters—including seasons 3 and 4! So grab your cart and head down each aisle to learn about Apple Blossom, Handbag Harriet, Suzie Sundae, Poppy Corn, and their friends. There's a world of fun in store, and it's time to start shopping. Check you later!

The produce aisle is the perfect place to play! The fruit and veggie Shopkins who hang out here know how to have a good time. They're bursting with personality, and there isn't a bad apple in the bunch!

# FRUIT & VEG

# APPLE BLOSSOM

**FAVORITE COLOR:**
Granny Smith green

**PERSONALITY:**
Sweet, tart, and a bit saucy

**SIGNATURE DANCE MOVE:**
The Worm

**FAVORITE VACATION DESTINATION:**
Mount Fuji

**FAVORITE WEATHER:**
A crisp fall day

**FIRST MEMORY:**
Sprouting from just a wee little seed

**QUOTE:**
"Check me out!"

At her core, Apple Blossom is sweet as pie and always up for adventure—she's ready to take a bite out of life!

**FAVORITE PASTIME:**
Chatting with pals on the vine

**AGE:**
Let's just say he's ripe!

**PRIZED POSSESSION:**
Family heirlooms

**KNOWN FOR:**
Being a seasoned storyteller

**BEST FRIEND:**
Gran Jam

***** **MISS MUSHY MOO** *****

**LIKES:**
Dark, damp places

**HOBBIES:**
Dirt-bike racing and making mud pies

**FAVORITE VACATION MEMORY:**
Antique shopping on Portobello Road

**BAD HABIT:**
She can sometimes have a big head.

**QUOTE:**
"There's a fungus among us!"

## ****** JUICY ORANGE ******

**LIKES:**
Juicy secrets

**DISLIKES:**
Rhyming

**KNOWN FOR:**
Her pithy jokes

**SPORTS SKILL:**
The squeeze play

## QUOTE:
"I'm juiced up and ready to go!"

## ****** CORNY COB ******

**LIKES:**
Puzzles and maizes

**PRIZED POSSESSION:**
Silk pajamas

**SIGNATURE DANCE MOVE:**
Pop-and-lock

**FAVORITE COLOR:**
Butter yellow

**BEST FEATURE:**
His husky voice

# STRAWBERRY KISS

**FAVORITE HOLIDAY:**
Valentine's Day

**BEST FRIEND:**
Apple Blossom

**FAVORITE SONG:**
"Strawberry Fields Forever"

**LIKES:**
Pink lemonade

**FAVORITE SINGER:**
Berry Manilow

**DREAMS ABOUT:**
What's in the strawberry patch at the end of the rainbow

 When Strawberry Kiss isn't lost in a daydream, you're sure to find her working on a new poem. Here's one she just finished! *Roses are red, violets are blue, Shopkins are sweet, and so are you!*

# ******* POSH PEAR *********

**PERSONALITY:**
Sweet, but a little spoiled

**FAVORITE ANIMAL:**
Partridge

**PERFECT ACCESSORY:**
Her pink "pear"
of sunglasses

**BEST FRIEND:**
Lippy Lips

## QUOTE:
"I can't help it if
I have appeal."

# **** PINEAPPLE CRUSH ****

**BEST VACATION
MEMORY:**
A luau in Hawaii

**CAN'T GET
ENOUGH OF:**
Fun in the sun

**HOBBIES:**
Sunbaking and hanging ten

**FAVORITE WEATHER:**
A tropical breeze

**KNOWN FOR:**
Her golden outlook on life

**LIMITED EDITION**

**KNOWN FOR:**
His concentration

**FAVORITE COLOR:**
Citron

**BEST FRIEND:**
Sour Lemon

**FAVORITE VACATION DESTINATION:**
The Florida Keys

**QUOTE:**
"Pucker up!"

***** CHLOE FLOWER ******

**HOBBY:**
Leafing through the newspaper

**BAD HABIT:**
Stalking out of a room when she's angry

**BEST FRIEND:**
Rockin' Broc

**PERSONAL HERO:**
Florets Nightingale

**QUOTE:**
"Let's veg out!"

## ★★★★★★ SWEET PEA ★★★★★★★

**NICKNAME:**
The Pod Squad

**BEST FRIEND:**
Cherrie Tomatoes

**GREATEST FEAR:**
Being alone

**FAVORITE HOBBY:**
Juggling

## QUOTE:
"Give peas a chance!"

## ★★★★★★★ PEACHY ★★★★★★★

**PERSONALITY:**
Sweet as pie

**KNOWN FOR:**
Her fuzzy memory

**HANGOUT:**
The ball pit

**FAVORITE VACATION DESTINATION:**
Georgia

**FAVORITE HOBBY:**
Chilling out with
Ice Cream Dream

# ***** CHEEKY CHERRIES ****

**NICKNAME:**
Double Trouble

**KNOWN FOR:**
Finishing each
other's sentences

**FAVORITE COLORS:**
Black and red

**BEST FRIEND:**
April Apricot

**NICKNAME:**
Maraschino Mamas

# ***** APRIL APRICOT ****

**DISLIKES:**
Wrinkles

**PERSONALITY:**
Fun and fruity

**SENSE OF HUMOR:**
Dry

**KNOWN FOR:**
Always getting in a jam

**QUOTE:**
"This is the pits!"

# AISLE 2
### Smells Delicious!

The Bakery aisle is always warm and inviting. These well-bread Shopkins make sure to savor the sweeter things in life. Feeling cozy around them is a piece of cake!

# BAKERY

**FAVORITE COLORS:**
Black and white

**GOOD AT:**
Thinking outside the cookie jar

**SPORTS SKILL:**
Dunking

**NICKNAME:**
Snickerdoodle

**KNOWN FOR:**
Milking a joke

**SECRET TALENT:**
Fortune-telling

**QUOTE:**
"My dad says I'm a chip off the old block!"

# KOOKY COOKIE

Kooky Cookie may be shy and a little crumbly around the edges, but her friends know she's very well-rounded.

**LIMITED EDITION**

***** DONNA DONUT ******

**HOBBY:**
Holing up with a good book

**FAVORITE WEATHER:**
A sprinkle of rain

**KNOWN FOR:**
Having dozens of friends

**FIRST MEMORY:**
Popping out of the oven

**FAVORITE SONG:**
"Dough-Re-Mi"

******* MINI MUFFIN *******

**FAVORITE MEAL:**
Brunch

**BEST TIME OF DAY:**
Morning. She's an early riser!

**SPORTS SKILL:**
Yoga, especially the sunrise salutation

**BEST FRIEND:**
Spilt Milk

**QUOTE:**
"Today is a bran-new day!"

# ***** SLICK BREADSTICK ****

**PERSONALITY:**
Crusty on the outside,
but warm on the inside

**FAVORITE HANGOUT:**
A Parisian café

**DISLIKES:**
Rain. It makes him feel soggy.

**BEST FRIENDS:**
Alpha Soup and Fasta Pasta

## QUOTE:
*"Zer is always time for
ze café break, no?"*

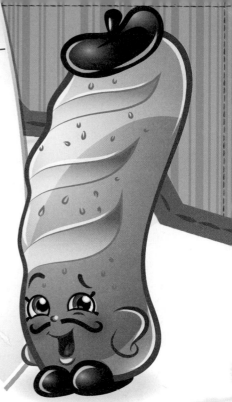

# ****** BREAD HEAD *******

**LIKES:**
Saving his dough

**DISLIKES:**
Stale jokes

**FAVORITE ACCESSORY:**
Loafers

**GREATEST FEAR:**
Getting sandwiched in a tight space

## QUOTE:
*"You're just buttering me up!"*

### *** CARRIE CARROT CAKE ***

**SIGNATURE DANCE MOVE:**
Raisin' the roof

**KNOWN FOR:**
Getting to the root of a problem

**PERSONALITY:**
Sweet but a little nutty

**PRIZED POSSESSION:**
Her 14-carrot gold ring

## QUOTE:
"As long as you have friends, everything else is just frosting."

### **** MARY MERINGUE *****

**KNOWN FOR:**
Whipping up treats

**BAD HABIT:**
Her sweet tooth

**PERSONALITY:**
She always has her head in the clouds.

**SECRET WEAPON:**
A dollop of courage

**HOMETOWN:**
Born and baked in Alaska

# D'LISH DONUT

**FAVORITE SPORT:**
Golf

**LOVES WHEN:**
There's a light frosting of snow on the ground

**HOBBY:**
Glazing pottery

**BEST FRIEND:**
Cheeky Chocolate

**BAD HABIT:**
Frittering the day away

**FAVORITE COLOR:**
Cinnamon brown

**QUOTE:**
"I *dough-know* what I'd do without my friends!"

 D'Lish Donut is the sportiest Shopkin around. She's filled with competitive spirit and always shoots for the perfect hole in one!

## ***** CHEESE LOUISE ******

**PERSONALITY:**
She may be rich, but she's very sweet.

**KNOWN FOR:**
Her New York style

**GOOD AT:**
Telling cheesy jokes

**FAVORITE COLOR:**
Chocolate brown

## QUOTE:
"Life is a cakewalk!"

## ****** PATTY CAKE *****

**LIKES:**
Birthday parties

**DISLIKES:**
Sharing

**BEST FRIEND:**
Cupcake Queen

**NICKNAME:**
Crumbs

## QUOTE:
"That's the icing on the cake!"

**KNOWN FOR:**
His dry sense
of humor

**HOBBY:**
Buttering up
his friends

# TOASTIE BREAD

**BEST FRIEND:**
Lana Banana Bread

**FAVORITE COLOR:**
White

**GOOD AT:**
Rising to the
occasion

**SPORTS SKILL:**
Putting some slice
on a tennis ball

**QUOTE:**
"If it's getting too hot,
it's time to pop!"

*Toastie Bread never loafs around. His hard work makes him the toast of the town!

# BAGEL BILLY

**KNOWN FOR:**
Laying it on thick

**PERSONALITY:**
Bagelicious

**LIKES:**
Everything

**FAVORITE WEATHER:**
Baking in the heat

**SIGNATURE DANCE MOVE:**
Roundhouse kick

**FAVORITE SONG:**
"Roll Over, Beethoven"

**QUOTE:**
"Open sesame!"

Bagel Billy is just plain wonderful. This well-rounded Shopkin will try anything—and he always goes the "hole" nine yards!

The seasoned Shopkins in the pantry aisle are full of flavor. But watch out! Some of them can be a bit wild and like to spice things up!

# PANTRY & INTERNATIONAL FOODS

# GRAN JAM

**FAVORITE COLOR:**
Raspberry pink

**SIGNATURE DANCE MOVE:**
The jelly roll

**HERO:**
Alexander the Grape

**HOBBIES:**
Knitting and jamming on the ukulele

**KNOWN FOR:**
Preserving memories in her scrapbook

**BAD HABIT:**
Stewing in her own juices

**QUOTE:**
"Aren't you a little sweetie?"

 This caring mama watches over all of Shopville. She spreads love and slathers affection on the Shopkins, sweetening their lives with her kind words.

# ****** SALLY SHAKES ******

**HER FRIENDS SAY:**
"Sally Shakes adds flavor to life!"

**DISLIKES:**
Unsavory characters

**SPORTS SKILL:**
The pinch hit

**HOBBY:**
Rock climbing

**FAVORITE BAND:**
The Spiced Girls

# ****** PEPPE PEPPER ******

**KNOWS HOW TO:**
Shake it on the dance floor

**WISHES HE:**
Could stop sneezing!

**COUSINS:**
Jalapeño, Cayenne, and Paprika

**BEST FRIEND:**
Sally Shakes.
They're rarely seen apart.

# QUOTE:
"Let's spice things up!"

# ******** HONEEEY *********

**HOBBIES:**
The spelling bee and catching flies

**GREATEST FEAR:**
Getting hives

**BEST FRIEND:**
Lee Tea

**LOVES TO:**
Comb the pages of
a good magazine

## QUOTE:
"What's the buzz?"

# ******** FI FI FLOUR ********

**KNOWN FOR:**
Being a bit of a mess

**LIKES:**
Half-baked ideas

**DISLIKES:**
Rolling pins and
feeling scattered

**FAVORITE
ACCESSORY:**
Her powder compact

## QUOTE:
"Flour power!"

**BREAKY CRUNCH**

**HOBBIES:**
Bowling and staying in shape

**LIKES:**
Surprise gifts

**DISLIKES:**
Flakes

**PERSONALITY:**
He goes against the grain.

**BEST FRIEND:**
Spilt Milk

**GREATEST FEAR:**
Getting soggy

**QUOTE:**
"Nothing can box me up!"

Breaky Crunch wakes up at the crack of dawn each morning and heads to the gym. Lifting weights and getting in a few crunches is the perfect way to start his day!

# **** LEE TEA ********

**LIKES:**
Handbags, shoulder bags,
and tea bags!

**DISLIKES:**
Steep prices

**FAVORITE ANIMAL:**
Teacup pig

**FAVORITE COLORS:**
Black and green

## QUOTE:
"I smell trouble brewing!"

# ****** SUGAR LUMP *******

**PERSONALITY:**
Sweet, but sometimes
a bit saccharine

**FAVORITE COLORS:**
Brown and white

**LIKES:**
Refined manners

**SECRET TALENT:**
Organization.
Storage cubes are her thing!

## QUOTE:
"There's nothing sweeter
than friendship."

# ****** FASTA PASTA *****

**FAVORITE ACCESSORY:**
His bow tie

**HOBBY:**
Noodling around on the piano

**PRIZED POSSESSION:**
His lucky "penne"

**SECRET WEAPON:**
Elbow grease

**PERSONAL HERO:**
His uncle Alfredo

# ****** TIN'A'TUNA *****

**LIMITED EDITION**

**FAVORITE SONG:**
"Roe, Roe, Roe Your Boat"

**LIKES:**
Swimming upstream

**DISLIKES:**
Canned applause

**FAVORITE CHARACTER:**
The Tin Man

**QUOTE:**
"Something's fishy!"

# TOMMY KETCHUP

**FAVORITE COLOR:**
Tomato red

**NICKNAME:**
Squirt

**LIKES:**
Zesty debates

**DISLIKES:**
Feeling drained

**BEST FRIEND:**
Frank Furter

**MAIN RIVAL:**
Cornell Mustard

**QUOTE:**
"Wait, guys!
Let me catch up!"

Tommy Ketchup is the perfect condiment-complement to any group. His friends relish hanging out with him, especially when he tells a saucy joke!

# ***** NETTI SPAGHETTI *****

**FAVORITE VACATION DESTINATION:**
Rome, Italy

**NICKNAME:**
Meatball

**BEST FRIEND:**
Sausage Sizzle

**BAD HABIT:**
Slurping her food

**SECRET TALENT:**
Twirling in ballet class

# ***** WALLY WATER ******

**FAVORITE COLOR:**
Aqua

**BAD HABIT:**
He can get boiling mad

**NICKNAME:**
$H_2O$

**SIGNATURE DANCE MOVE:**
The Sprinkler

**FAVORITE HANGOUT:**
Chilling at the pool

# TACO TERRIE

**PERSONALITY:**
A little bit crunchy

**BEST FRIEND:**
Lammy Lamington

**FAVORITE VACATION DESTINATION:**
Cancún, Mexico

**FAVORITE WEATHER:**
Hot! Hot! Hot!

**HOBBY:**
Salsa dancing

**BAD HABIT:**
Falling apart under pressure

**QUOTE:**
"¡Ay, caramba!"

 Taco Terrie may be full of beans, but he's the life of every party. When there is a fiesta, this spicy señor has no time for a siesta!

This is the aisle where everyone in Shopville likes to kick back and chill out. All are welcome—the dairy and frozen food Shopkins don't give anyone the cold shoulder!

# DAIRY & FROZEN FOOD

**LIKES:**
Taking center stage

**BEST FRIENDS:**
Freezy Peazy and
Cheezey B

**HIS FRIENDS SAY:**
"Chee Zee can be
a bit crackers."

**FAVORITE SCARY MOVIE:**
Frankenstein's
Muenster

**FAVORITE VACATION DESTINATION:**
The Swiss Alps

**GREATEST FEAR:**
Mice

**QUOTE:**
"Gouda been better.
Let's try it again!"

Chee Zee has a secret talent—he writes original rap songs! Check out his latest beats: *My name is Chee Zee, I'm bold and breezy, but don't try to squeeze me, or else I'll get freezy!*

# ******* BUTTERCUP ***

**SECRET TALENT:**
He has great taste!

**FIRST MEMORY:**
Being whipped into shape

**FAVORITE COLOR:**
Mellow yellow

**PERSONALITY:**
Rich, but never spoiled

**HIS FRIENDS SAY:**
"Buttercup will melt your heart!"

**LIMITED EDITION**

# ***** FREEZY PEAZY ******

**FAVORITE WEATHER:**
Snow

**FIRST MEMORY:**
Leaving the pod

**PET PEEVE:**
Bad manners.
He minds his p's and q's.

**FAVORITE RAPPER:**
Master P

## QUOTE:

"Be cool!"

## \*\*\*\*\*\*\* POPSI COOL \*\*\*\*\*\*\*\*

**LOVES TO:**
Chill out

**FUN FACT:**
Rumor has it she has a twin.

**HOBBIES:**
Ice-skating and sledding

**GREATEST FEAR:**
Freezer burn

## QUOTE:

"I can lick any problem!"

## \*\*\*\*\*\*\*\*\*\*\* YO-CHI \*\*\*\*\*\*\*\*\*\*

**HOBBY:**
Swirling around
the dance floor

**FAVORITE POP
MUSIC ARTIST:**
Vanilla Ice Cream

**PERSONALITY:**
Well-cultured

**FASHION STYLE:**
She's always sporting
a new topping.

## QUOTE:

"Every day should have a
different flavor!"

# SPILT MILK

**KNOWN FOR:**
Being a bit of a klutz

**HOBBY:**
Skimming through comic books

**FAVORITE VACATION DESTINATION:**
Wisconsin

**PERSONALITY:**
He sometimes cries over the little things.

**FAVORITE WEATHER:**
Pouring rain

**DISLIKES:**
Spoiled people really get him steamed!

**BEST JOKE:**
"What do you get from an Alaskan cow? *Ice cream!*"

You'll never be bored with Spilt Milk around! He's half silly and half serious, and he really likes to stir things up!

There's always a reason to celebrate with these rockin' Shopkins. Whether it's someone's birthday, a holiday, or just an average Tuesday, they'll find something that deserves a special treat!

# PARTY FOOD & SWEET TREATS

## RAINBOW BITE

**STYLE SECRET:**
Any color looks good on her.

**BEST FRIEND:**
Soda Pops

**PERSONAL HERO:**
Roy G. Biv

**HOBBIES:**
Painting

## QUOTE:
"You need a little rain to get a rainbow!"

## SODA POPS

**PERSONALITY:**
Super-bubbly

**DISLIKES:**
Being shaken up

**BAD HABIT:**
Too much caffeine

**HOBBY:**
Refreshing her wardrobe

## QUOTE:
"I hate to burst your bubble . . ."

## ********* WISHES *********

**AGE:**
A year worth celebrating!

**PRIZED POSSESSION:**
Candles from her first birthday

**FAVORITE SONG:**
"When You Wish Upon a Star"

**KNOWN FOR:**
Throwing surprise parties

## QUOTE:
"You *can* have your cake and eat it, too!"

## ******** WOBBLES *********

**LIKES:**
Wiggling to a good beat

**FAVORITE SONG:**
"Getting Jiggly With It"

**PERSONALITY:**
A worrier who bounces from problem to problem

**PET PEEVE:**
It feels like her friends can see right through her.

**MOTTO:**
Dancing shakes the stress away.

## ****** LOLLI POPPINS ******

**PERSONALITY:**
Sweet, but a little hard
to get along with

**BAD HABIT:**
She's stuck in her ways.

**DISLIKES:**
Lollygagging around

**BEST FRIEND:**
Candi Cotton

## QUOTE:
"I'm no sucker!"

## ****** BUBBLES ********

**LIKES:**
A good chat-'n'-chew
with friends

**KNOWN FOR:**
Bursting into song

**SPORTS SKILL:**
Pop fly

**BAD HABIT:**
Flapping her gums

**FAVORITE MOVIE
CHARACTER:**
Chewbacca

# CHEEKY CHOCOLATE

**BEST PRANK:**
Convincing her friends she's melted

**FAVORITE ANIMAL:**
Chocolate Labrador

**KNOWN FOR:**
Breaking out laughing

**BEST FRIENDS:**
D'Lish Donut and Apple Blossom

**FAVORITE VACATION DESTINATION:**
Hershey, Pennsylvania

**HOBBIES:**
Pulling pranks and melting hearts

**QUOTE:**
"Oops!
I spilled the beans!"

Cheeky Chocolate loves to laugh. She's a prankster who isn't afraid of getting her hands dirty!

### *** ICE CREAM DREAM ***

**BEST FRIEND:**
Waffle Sue

**PET PEEVE:**
Brain freeze

**PERSONALITY:**
She can be a bit drippy.

**NICKNAME:**
Half-Pint

**PRIZED POSSESSION:**
A sterling silver scoop

### ****** MARSHA MELLOW *****

**HER FRIENDS SAY:**
"She's a real softie!"

**BEST FRIEND:**
Choco Lava

**DISLIKES:**
Being too hot.
It makes her feel puffy.

**LOVES TO:**
Tell stories by
the campfire

**QUOTE:**
"Let's play s'more!"

LIMITED EDITION

# **** TWINKY WINKS ****

### EARLIEST MEMORY:
Being just a wee Shopkin
in a snuggly wrapper

### PERSONALITY:
She's full of surprises.

### BAD HABIT:
Sponging off of her friends

### DISLIKES:
Needing fillings at the dentist

## QUOTE:
"Shopkins are the
cream of the crop!"

# ****** LE'QUORICE ******

### PERSONALITY:
Some say she's an acquired taste.

### FAVORITE GAME:
Hopscotch

### HER FRIENDS KNOW:
She'll always stick by them.

### FASHION STYLE:
Colorful layers

### BEST FRIEND:
Mandy Candy

## ***** CUPCAKE QUEEN *****

**FAVORITE COLOR:**
Buttercream

**ENJOYS:**
Hosting grand balls

**FAVORITE ACCESSORY:**
A crown of frosting

**PRIZED POSSESSION:**
Red-velvet slippers

**DREAMS ABOUT:**
Becoming royalty

LIMITED EDITION

## ***** POPPY CORN ******

**HOBBY:**
Going to the movies

**SPORTS SKILL:**
None—he's a real butterfingers!

**HAS A TENDENCY TO:**
Pop up unexpectedly

**HALLOWEEN COSTUME:**
An army kernel

**QUOTE:**
"I've got this in the bag!"

# SUZIE SUNDAE

**FAVORITE MOVIE:**
Frozen

**FAVORITE COLOR:**
Cherry red

**FAVORITE FOOD:**
She's nuts about ice cream

**HOBBIES:**
Relaxing on a Sunday

**SIGNATURE DANCE MOVE:**
The Splits

**BEST FRIEND:**
Ice Cream Dream

**QUOTE:**
"Pretty please . . . with a cherry on top?"

Suzie Sundae is a Shopkin with a lot of glass! And if you want to have fun, there's no topping a day with Suzie!

## ****** MACCA ROON *******

**PERSONALITY:**
One colorful character

**FAVORITE HANGOUT:**
Sandwiched between
two good friends

**SIGNATURE DANCE MOVE:**
Pirouette

**FAVORITE VACATION DESTINATION:**
The Eiffel Tower

**QUOTE:**
"Ooh, la la!"

## ****** CANDY APPLE ******

**PERSONALITY:**
Dependable. She'll always
stick with you!

**FAVORITE HANGOUT:**
The county fair

**LIKES:**
Hayrides and merry-go-rounds

**KNOWN FOR:**
Getting into sticky situations

**GREATEST FEAR:**
Going to the dentist

**LIKES:**
Surprises

**SECRET TALENT:**
Rapping

**PERSONALITY:**
Giving

**PET PEEVE:**
Forgotten birthdays

**FAVORITE SPORT:**
Boxing

**FAVORITE ACCESSORY:**
Ribbons and bows

**QUOTE:**
"Sharing is caring!"

# MISS PRESSY

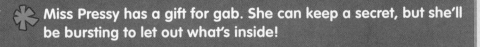

Miss Pressy has a gift for gab. She can keep a secret, but she'll be bursting to let out what's inside!

# ******* KYLIE CONE *********

**FAVORITE COLOR:**
Cream

**BAD HABIT:**
Waffling on and on

**FAVORITE SPORT:**
Ice hockey

**NICKNAME:**
Sugar

**FAVORITE WEATHER:**
Drippy

# **** BERRY SMOOTHIE ****

**PERSONALITY:**
Cool and fresh

**FAVORITE COLOR:**
Blue

**BEST FRIEND:**
Pancake Jake

**HIDDEN TALENT:**
Can blend into a crowd

## QUOTE:
"Looks like it's smooth sailing!"

# PANCAKE JAKE

**LIKES:**
Reading the Sunday newspaper

**FAVORITE TREE:**
Maple

**KNOWN FOR:**
Flipping over backward to help his friends

**FAVORITE CHARACTERS:**
Flapjack and Jill

**QUOTE:**
"Batter up!"

**BAD HABIT:**
When he sings, he's a little flat.

**FAVORITE VACATION DESTINATION:**
Vermont

Wake up and say good morning to Pancake Jake!
He's a stack of fun and totally pantastic!

# AISLE 6
## Scrub-a-Dub!

The cleaning and laundry aisle is super fresh. The tidy Shopkins who hang out here make a game out of putting things in order. And they never play dirty!

# CLEANING & LAUNDRY

**SPORTS SKILL:**
Mopping the floor with the competition

**FAVORITE SONG:**
"Whistle While You Work"

**HER FRIENDS SAY:**
"Molly can wring out any problem!"

**KNOWN FOR:**
Her strong work ethic

**ENJOYS:**
Checking things off her bucket list

**LIKES:**
Seeing her reflection in a clean, shiny floor

**SECRET TALENT:**
Getting a handle on the situation

# MOLLY MOPS

 This hardworking miss knows how to get the job done. But don't be fooled by her can-do attitude—she's buckets of fun!

********** LEAFY **********

**FAVORITE SONG:**
"Wipeout"

**SIGNATURE DANCE MOVE:**
The Tootsie Roll

**LIKES TO:**
Unwind with a good magazine

**DISLIKES:**
Feeling flushed

**QUOTE:**
"Let the good times roll!"

**LIMITED EDITION**

***** RUB-A-GLOVE **

**KNOWN FOR:**
Dishing the dirt

**HOBBY:**
Water sports

**BEST FRIEND:**
Molly Mops

**PRIZED POSSESSION:**
Rubber duck

**QUOTE:**
"Can you give me a hand?"

# SQUEAKY CLEAN

**PERSONALITY:**
Honest and clean-cut

**LIKES:**
Water slides and bubble baths

**DISLIKES:**
Airing dirty laundry in public

**BEST FRIEND:**
Leafy

**SECRET WEAPON:**
The sparkle in his eye

**KNOWN FOR:**
Cleaning house

**QUOTE:**
"Neat-o!"

Squeaky Clean always does what's right. He likes to try new things, but he isn't afraid to clean up after his own messes.

Welcome to Aisle 7, where the friendly homewares Shopkins are always eager for company! They're sure to make anyone feel right at home.

# BABY, HOMEWARES & STATIONERY

# DUM MEE MEE

**AGE:**
Just a tyke

**FAVORITE SINGER:**
Lady Goo-Goo-Ga-Ga

**FAVORITE COLOR:**
Baby blue

**SECRET TALENT:**
Keeping the peace—
she's a pacifier!

**BEST FRIEND:**
Sippy Sips

**FAVORITE FLOWER:**
Baby's breath

## QUOTE:
"You'll never cry when I'm around."

Dum Mee Mee is a little cutie who was born to shop. She may be tiny, but she's got a very big heart.

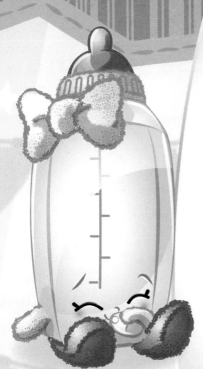

## ******** DRIBBLES ********

**PERSONALITY:**
She can be
rather formulaic.

**RELAXES BY:**
Reheating in a nice,
warm bath

**LIKES:**
Nursery rhymes

**DISLIKES:**
People who bottle
up their emotions

**LOOKS UP TO:**
Sippy Sips

## ****** SIPPY SIPS ********

**KNOWN FOR:**
Never spilling a secret

**FAVORITE
SPORTING EVENT:**
The World Cup

**ENJOYS:**
Singing lullabies before bedtime

**PRIZED POSSESSION:**
A stuffed bear

## QUOTE:

"Enjoy life one sip at a time."

# ★★★★★★★ LANA LAMP ★★★★★★★

**FAVORITE TIME OF DAY:**
Bright and early

**BEST FEATURE:**
Her smile has serious wattage.

**PERSONALITY:**
Brilliant

**KNOWN FOR:**
Always looking on the bright side

## QUOTE:
"We've got it made in the shade!"

# ★★★ BRENDA BLENDER ★★★★

**LIKES:**
Stirring up trouble

**DISLIKES:**
Blending in

**PERSONALITY:**
She's a real smoothie operator!

**DREAMS ABOUT:**
Having superpowers

## QUOTE:
"Let's mix it up!"

# TOASTY POP

**HOBBIES:**
Throwing parties and giving toasts

**KNOWN FOR:**
Never having a stale idea

**DISLIKES:**
Burning out

**ISN'T AFRAID:**
To grab a slice of life

**BEST FRIEND:**
Buttercup

**FAVORITE WEATHER:**
Dry heat

**QUOTE:**
"Let's get cookin'!"

 The only things warmer than Toasty Pop's personality are his words. When he gives a speech, there isn't a dry eye in the house.

# CHATTER

**BEST FEATURE:**
She's never at a loss for words!

**FAVORITE GAME:**
Telephone

**PET PEEVE:**
A busy signal

**SECRET TALENT:**
Pushing people's buttons

**BEST FRIEND:**
Mobile Mary

**QUOTE:**
"Call me!"

Chatter is dialed in to the latest gossip and loves to spread the word. Whether she's talking shop or just making chitchat, she always has a kind word for all her friends.

# ***** FROST T FRIDGE *****

**PERSONALITY:**
Super-chill

**LIKES:**
Feeling full

**FAVORITE WEATHER:**
Cold and crisp

**BAD HABIT:**
Leaving the door open
and the lights on

**QUOTE:**
"I'm keepin' it cool!"

# ****** COMFY CHAIR ******

**HOBBY:**
Curling up with a good book

**PERSONALITY:**
A big softie

**FAVORITE VACATION
DESTINATION:**
The Big Easy (New Orleans)

**FAVORITE GAME:**
Musical chairs

**QUOTE:**
"Let's get rocking!"

**GOOD AT:**
Getting in touch with her roots

**BEST FRIEND:**
Mintee

**FASHION STYLE:**
Flowers everywhere

**FAVORITE VACATION DESTINATION:**
The Garden State (New Jersey)

**BIGGEST FEAR:**
A frosty day

**KNOWN FOR:**
Rosy cheeks

**FAVORITE COLOR:**
Violet

# PETA PLANT

Peta Plant is a true nature girl who tries to grow a little every day. She's always ready for an outdoor adventure!

**SPORTS SKILL:**
Channel surfing

**LIKES:**
When everyone is looking at her

**BEST COSTUME:**
Rabbit ears

**PERSONALITY:**
Plugged in

**QUOTE:**
"I'm all about the drama!"

**** PENNY PENCIL ********

**PERSONALITY:**
Her happiness rubs off on others

**HOBBIES:**
Writing and drawing

**NICKNAME:**
Number 2

**BAD HABIT:**
Reaching her
breaking point

**QUOTE:**
"Write on!"

## ****** ERICA ERASER ******

**KNOWN FOR:**
Performing magic—she loves
to make things disappear

**FAVORITE COLOR:**
Pink

**BEST FRIEND:**
Penny Pencil

**BAD HABIT:**
She's easily rubbed
the wrong way.

**LIKES:**
New beginnings

## ******* SECRET SALLY ******

**PERSONALITY:**
She's pretty private.

**DISLIKES:**
Loudmouths

**GOOD AT:**
Remembering old times

**FAVORITE HOBBY:**
Playing hide and secret

## QUOTE:
"My lips are sealed!"

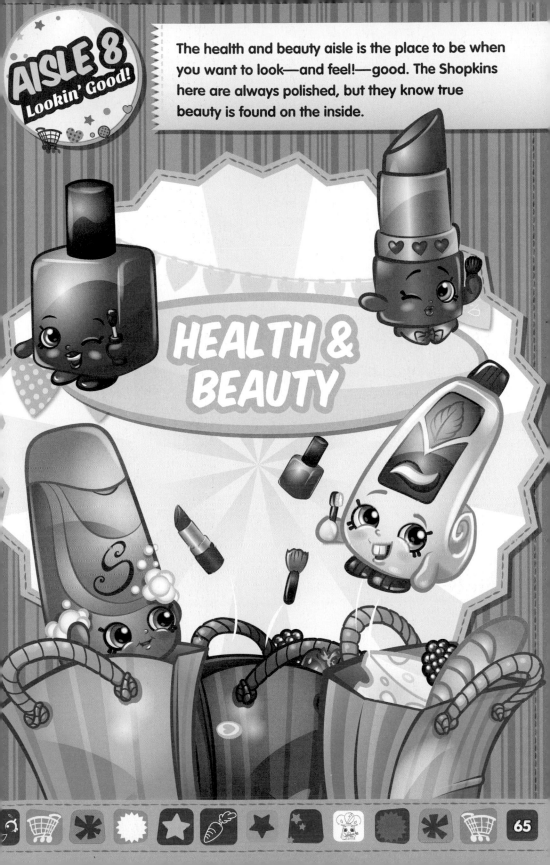

# AISLE 8
## Lookin' Good!

The health and beauty aisle is the place to be when you want to look—and feel!—good. The Shopkins here are always polished, but they know true beauty is found on the inside.

# HEALTH & BEAUTY

# LIPPY LIPS

**PERSONALITY:**
Sassy and
a bit bossy

**STYLE SENSE:**
She has a different
shade for every mood

**BEST FRIENDS:**
Apple Blossom and
Polly Polish

**LIKES:**
Glossy magazines

**DISLIKES:**
Dull colors

**HOBBIES:**
Acting and
shopping

**QUOTE:**
"Have a
beautiful day!"

There's one word to describe this fashionista:
*beautiful.* Lippy Lips lives to shop, loves to gab,
and leaves her mark wherever she goes!

# ✳✳✳✳✳✳✳ POLLY POLISH ✳✳✳✳✳✳✳

**PERSONALITY:**
A risk-taker

**STYLE SENSE:**
She loves trying new colors.

**KNOWN FOR:**
Telling the unvarnished truth

**DISLIKES:**
Chips

**QUOTE:**
"Nailed it!"

# ✳✳✳✳✳✳✳ SCRUBS ✳✳✳✳✳✳✳✳✳

**BEST FEATURE:**
I lis pearly-white smile

**PRIZED POSSESSION:**
A golden toothbrush

**FAVORITE COLOR:**
Mint green

**FAVORITE STORYBOOK CHARACTER:**
The Cheshire Cat

**QUOTE:**
"Keep on smiling!"

## ******** SHAMPY *********

**PERSONALITY:**
Bubbly and stylish

**BAD HABIT:**
Getting worked up into a lather

**FAVORITE WEATHER:**
Rain showers

**BEST FEATURE:**
She always smells fresh.

**SIGNATURE DANCE MOVE:**
The Wave

## ********* SILKY *********

**PERSONALITY:**
A smooth operator

**PET PEEVE:**
A bad hair day

**DISLIKES:**
Hot weather.
It makes her feel frizzy.

**BEST FRIEND:**
Shampy

**LOVES:**
Swimming and day spas

**FAVORITE VACATION DESTINATION:**
Miami Beach

**FAVORITE WEATHER:**
The hotter the better!

**FAVORITE COLOR:**
Ultraviolet

**PERFECT ACCESSORY:**
Her sunglasses, of course

**ENJOYS:**
A coconut-banana smoothie

**QUOTE:**
"Life is a day at the beach!"

# SUNNY SCREEN

LIMITED EDITION

SPF 30+

Sunny Screen can be a bit of a worrier, but deep down she just wants to take care of her friends. No one's getting burned on her watch!

# ****** MINDY MIRROR *****

**KNOWN FOR:**
Her compact size

**PERSONALITY:**
Reflective and thoughtful

**HERO:**
Snow White

**GREATEST FEAR:**
Seven years of bad luck

## QUOTE:
"Here's looking at you!"

# ******* BLUSHY BRUSH *****

**PERSONALITY:**
A little cheeky

**GOOD AT:**
Making up
after a fight

**BEST FRIEND:**
Mindy Mirror

**FAVORITE COLOR:**
Pink

## QUOTE:
"Color me happy!"

# **** FRENCHY PERFUME ****

**PERSONALITY:**
A true romantic

**DREAM PET:**
French bulldog

**FASHION STYLE:**
Trés chic!

**FAVORITE VACATION DESTINATION:**
Cologne, France

**QUOTE:**
"Oui, oui!"

LIMITED EDITION

LIMITED EDITION

# **** GEMMA BOTTLE *****

**PERSONALITY:**
Ab-scent minded

**LIKES:**
The sweet smell
of success

**PRIZED POSSESSION:**
Crystal ball

**FAVORITE COLOR:**
Rainbow

**KNOWN FOR:**
Her fragrant
garden

# **** PRETTY BOW KAY ****

**FAVORITE HOLIDAY:**
Mother's Day

**PERSONALITY:**
Light and airy

**DECORATING TIP:**
Put a bow on it!

**HOBBY:**
Makeovers at
the mall

**SECRET TALENT:**
Sniffing out a deal

# ***** PRETTY PUFF *****

**HOBBY:**
Entering beauty
pageants

**FAVORITE WEATHER:**
Misty

**DREAMS ABOUT:**
The ocean spray

**HOBBY:**
Aerobics

# QUOTE:

*"I smell trouble!"*

## ****** SALLY SCENT ******

**LIMITED EDITION**

**PERSONALITY:**
Strong and sweet

**BEST FRIEND:**
Candy Kisses

**FAVORITE HOLIDAY:**
Valentine's Day

**LOVES READING:**
Romance novels

**BEST FEATURE:**
Her nose for news

## **** SPARKLY SPRITZ ****

**LIMITED EDITION**

**SPORTS SKILL:**
Playing short stopper

**FAVORITE SONG:**
"Twinkle, Twinkle,
Little Star"

**HOBBY:**
Aromatherapy

**DREAMS ABOUT:**
Catching lightning in a bottle

**BEST FEATURE:**
Everyone takes a
shine to her.

You can find all of the most fashionable Shopkins in the accessory aisle. They look great from head to toe because they know the real secret to style: A beautiful heart!

# SHOES, HATS & ACCESSORIES

# ***** BUN BUN SLIPPER ****

**SIGNATURE DANCE MOVE:**
The bunny hop

**PRIZED POSSESSION:**
Lucky rabbit's foot

**PERFECT ACCESSORY:**
Her cozy bathrobe

**PERSONAL HERO:**
The Easter Bunny

## QUOTE:
"I'll go toe-to-toe
with anyone!"

# ****** SNEAKY WEDGE *****

**PERSONALITY:**
Footloose and
fancy-free

**BAD HABIT:**
Lying about
her height

**FAVORITE HANGOUT:**
The gym

**SECRET TALENT:**
She can be
very sneaky.

## \*\*\*\*\*\*\*\* PROMMY \*\*\*\*\*\*\*\*\*

**LIKES:**
Getting dressed up
for special occasions

**PERSONALITY:**
High-spirited, never flat

**KNOWN FOR:**
Her fabulous style sense

**HOBBY:**
Kicking up her heels

**QUOTE:**
"You can never look
too gorgeous!"

## \*\*\*\* ANGIE ANKLE BOOT \*\*\*

LIMITED
EDITION

**NICKNAME:**
Tootsie

**KNOWN FOR:**
Taking problems in stride

**PERSONALITY:**
Practical, yet sleek

**FAVORITE ACCESSORY:**
Leg warmers

**QUOTE:**
"Don't go getting too
big for your boots!"

# SNEAKY SALLY

**SPORTS SKILL:**
Fancy footwork

**GOOD AT:**
Solving knotty problems

**LIKES:**
Being a step ahead of her friends

**BEST FRIEND:**
Kelly Jelly

**DISLIKES:**
Unsporting behavior

**BAD HABIT:**
Sticking her tongue out

## QUOTE:
"If you don't try, you can't win!"

Sneaky Sally is laced up and ready for action. She's got a competitive spirit and the sole of a champion.

## ********* HEELY **********

**SIGNATURE DANCE MOVE:**
The two-step

**FAVORITE ANIMAL:**
Kitten

**BEST FRIEND:**
Prommy

**FAVORITE VACATION DESTINATION:**
Fashion Week in Paris

## QUOTE:
"I'll keep you on your toes!"

## ******** KELLY JELLY ******

**PERSONALITY:**
A kid at heart

**FAVORITE SPORT:**
Jelly wrestling

**BEST QUALITY:**
Being totally transparent

**SIGNATURE DANCE MOVE:**
The Grapevine

## QUOTE:
"Do I make myself clear?"

**KNOWN FOR:**
Keeping everyone in stitches!

**SIGNATURE DANCE MOVE:**
The Moonwalk

**BEST FRIEND:**
Penny Purse

**FAVORITE SONG:**
"Heart and Sole"

**PRIZED POSSESSION:**
Her grandmother's quilt

**FAVORITE MOVIE:**
Happy Feet

**QUOTE:**
"These boots were made for walking!"

# QUILTY BOOT

Quilty Boot loves to dance up a storm! When she's not teaching the Shopkins all the latest steps, she's groovin' to the music she feels deep down in her sole!

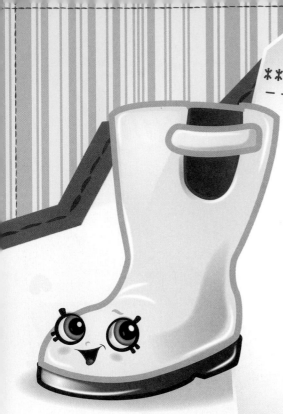

## ***** JENNIFER RAYNE ******

**DISLIKES:**
Wet blankets

**FAVORITE HOBBY:**
Splashing in puddles

**BAD HABIT:**
Always up to her ankles in trouble

**FAVORITE COLOR:**
Yellow

**QUOTE:**
"Whatever you do, make a splash!"

## ****** TAYLOR RAYNE *****

**PERSONALITY:**
Slicker than most

**KNOWN FOR:**
Chasing rainbows

**BEST FRIEND:**
Her sister, Jennifer Rayne

**SPORTS SKILL:**
The hat trick

**SIGNATURE DANCE MOVE:**
The head bop

# CASPER CAP

**NICKNAME:**
Ten-Gallon

**DISLIKES:**
Helmet hair

**FAVORITE HOBBY:**
Baseball

**BEST FRIEND:**
Floppy Cap

**SECRET TALENT:**
An excellent bowler

**FAVORITE VACATION DESTINATION:**
Panama

**QUOTE:**
"Keep a lid on it!"

Hat's off to Casper Cap! He can cap off any outfit and is always in peak condition. In fact, he's head and shoulders above the rest!

# HANDBAG HARRIET

**LIKES:**
Getting carried away

**DISLIKES:**
Empty wallets

**BEST FEATURE:**
Pursed lips

**BAD HABIT:**
Keeping everything inside

**SPORTS SKILL:**
Clutch shots at the buzzer

**NICKNAME:**
Pocket Bookworm

**QUOTE:**
"I've got this in the bag!"

Handbag Harriet is always prepared to handle anything. She's got all of life's necessities: money, snacks, tissues . . . and lots of laughs!

******** ROXY RING ********

**PERSONALITY:**
Sparkling

**HOBBY:**
Attending weddings

**SIGNATURE DANCE MOVE:**
The Finger Tap

**FAVORITE COLOR:**
Sapphire blue

**QUOTE:**
"I'm a cut above the rest!"

*** RING-A-ROSIE *****

**LIKES:**
Rock bands

**BEST FEATURE:**
Always looks for
the silver lining!

**BEST FRIEND:**
Roxy Ring

**FAVORITE COLOR:**
Ruby red

**FAVORITE GAME:**
Ring-Around-
the-Rosy

# TICKY TOCK

**LIMITED EDITION**

**PERSONALITY:**
Organized and punctual

**BEST FEATURE:**
Quick hands

**FAVORITE POEM:**
"Hickory Dickory Dock"

**PET PEEVE:**
Running late

**FAVORITE HOBBY:**
Watching time go by

**BAD HABIT:**
Getting too wound up

**QUOTE:**
"Time is on my side!"

Things always run like clockwork with Ticky Tock around. It takes time to get to know her, but once you do the seconds will fly by.

# CHELSEA CHARM

**KNOWN FOR:** Being lucky

**FAVORITE FICTIONAL CHARACTER:** Prince Charming

**FASHION STYLE:** Her outfits always match!

**BEST FRIEND:** Ticky Tock

**FAVORITE HOBBY:** Hanging with her BFF

**DISLIKES:** Broken hearts

**QUOTE:** "Best Friends Forever!"

LIMITED EDITION

Chelsea Charm lives a charmed life. Whether she's brightening up the day or just hanging around, she's a good friend who isn't afraid to show it!

# ***** RUBY EARRING ******

**PERSONALITY:**
A diamond in the rough

**FAVORITE COLOR:**
Emerald green

**BAD HABIT:**
Leaving her friends dangling

**SPORTS SKILL:**
Hanging ten

**FAVORITE HOBBY:**
Getting hooked on something new

---

# **** BRENDA BROOCH ***

**LIKES:**
Being worn out

**BEST FRIEND:**
Ruby Earring

**KNOWN FOR:**
Throwing dinner parties

**FASHION STYLE:**
Neat as a pin

# QUOTE:
"Shine on!"

# PENNY PURSE

**LIKES:** Coining new phrases

**DISLIKES:** Change

**HEROES:** Abraham Lincoln and George Washington

**PET PEEVE:** Getting stuck with the bill

**FAVORITE COLORS:** Silver and gold

**FASHION STYLE:** Pockets everywhere

**QUOTE:** "My money's on you!"

She's always a tissue, a mirror, or a shoulder to lean on for all of her friends!

The Petkins aisle is the perfect place to find Shopkins' best friends. Whether they're learning new tricks or barking up the wrong tree, the Petkins are perfect animal companions!

# PETKINS

# BONE-ADETTE

**FAVORITE HANGOUT:**
The butcher shop

**KNOWN FOR:**
Biting off more than she can chew

**FAVORITE COLOR:**
Milky white

**DREAMS ABOUT:**
Buried treasure

**SPORTS SKILL:**
The doggy paddle

**HOBBY:**
Bird-watching and chasing cars

**FAVORITE WEATHER:**
The dog days of summer

Bone-adette is one funny bone who's always yappy—except when she's buried by her dog friends.

## ***** FISH FLAKE JAKE *****

**SIGNATURE DANCE MOVE:**
The Swim

**FAVORITE HOBBIES:**
Swimming and eating

**BEST FRIEND:**
Goldie Fish Bowl

**FAVORITE VEHICLE:**
Tank

**BAD HABIT:**
Flaking on his friends

## ********** SHY PIE *********

**FAVORITE VACATION DESTINATION:**
A desert island

**BAD HABIT:**
Falling to pieces

**FAVORITE HOLIDAY:**
The Fourth of July

**PERSONALITY:**
Sweet and loyal—a Shopkin you can always crust!

**FASHION STYLE:**
Loves gingham

# HOT CHOC

**LIKES:**
Fairy tails

**DISLIKES:**
Cat-astrophes

**BEST FRIEND:**
Milk Bud

**PERSONALITY:**
Warm and welcoming

**BEST FEATURE:**
Her sweet purr

**HERO:**
Coco Chanel

## QUOTE:
"Meow!"

Hot Choc is the purr-fect companion. This Petkin loves to play, but she also enjoys snuggling on cold, blustery days.

## ******** MILK BUD ********

**LIKES:**
Cuddling

**DISLIKES:**
Curdling

**FAVORITE HOBBY:**
Making moosic

**FAVORITE JOKE:**
"What do you call
a magical cow?
The Dairy Fairy!"

## ****** RITA REMOTE ******

**PERSONALITY:**
Controlled

**DISLIKES:**
When people push her buttons

**FAVORITE COLOR:**
Anything muted

**KNOWN FOR:**
Constantly changing her tune

**FAVORITE VACATION
DESTINATION:**
The English Channel

**LIKES:**
Taking a cat nap

**FAVORITE COLOR:**
Green

**BAD HABIT:**
Sinking his claws in

**FAVORITE WEATHER:**
Pouring rain

**SIGNATURE DANCE MOVE:**
The Cancan

**FAVORITE SONG:**
"I'm a Little Teapot"

**QUOTE:**
"Meow!"

# DRIPS

 Drips can be silly and very spilly, but he loves to help in the garden (and lie in the sunshine!).

# COLLECTOR'S SHOPPING LIST

○ COMMON
● RARE
● ULTRA RARE
● SPECIAL EDITION

CHECK OFF YOUR COLLECTED SHOPKINS TO SEE WHICH ONES YOU STILL HAVE TO FIND!

## FINISHES:

 **GLITTER SHOPKINS**

**FROZEN SHOPKINS**

**METALLIC SHOPKINS**

**BLING SHOPKINS**

**FLUFFY BABY SHOPKINS**

 There are so many Shopkins to check out. Use this list to collect the whole bunch!

::::::::::SEASON 1:::::::::::
******* PANTRY *******

| | | | |
|---|---|---|---|
| Tommy Ketchup 1-015 ○ | Nutty Butter 1-016 ● | Peppe Pepper 1-017 ○ | Sally Shakes 1-018 ○ |
| Sugar Lump 1-019 ● | Breaky Crunch 1-020 ● | Alpha Soup 1-021 ○ | Gran Jam 1-022 ○ |
| Coolio 1-023 ○ | Tommy Ketchup 1-024 ○ | Nutty Butter 1-025 ○ | Peppe Pepper 1-026 ○ |
| Sally Shakes 1-027 ● | Sugar Lump 1-028 ● | Breaky Crunch 1-029 ● | Alpha Soup 1-030 ○ |
| Gran Jam 1-031 ○ | Coolio 1-032 ○ | | |

:::::::::SEASON 2:::::::::::
******* PANTRY *******

| | | | |
|---|---|---|---|
| Fi Fi Flour 2-069 ● | Bart Beans 2-070 ○ | Fasta Pasta 2-071 ○ | Olivia Oil 2-072 ● |
| Honeeey 2-073 ● | Al Foil 2-074 ○ | Toffy Coffee 2-075 ○ | Cornell Mustard 2-076 ○ |
| Chris P Crackers 2-077 ○ | Fi Fi Flour 2-078 ○ | Bart Beans 2-079 ○ | Fasta Pasta 2-080 ○ |
| Olivia Oil 2-081 ● | Honeeey 2-082 ○ | Al Foil 2-083 ○ | Toffy Coffee 2-084 ○ |
| Cornell Mustard 2-085 ○ | Chris P Crackers 2-086 ○ | | |

::::::::::SEASON 1::::::::::
****** FRUIT & VEG ******

Apple Blossom 1-001 ⚪
Rockin' Broc 1-002 ⚪
Strawberry Kiss 1-003 ⚪
Pineaple Crush 1-004 ⚪

Melonie Pips 1-005 ⚫
Miss Mushy Moo 1-006 ⚪
Posh Pear 1-007 ⚪
Apple Blossom 2-008 ⚪

Rockin' Broc 1-009 ⚪
Strawberry Kiss 1-010 ⚫
Pineapple Crush 1-011 ⚪
Melonie Pips 1-012 ⚫

Miss Musshy-Moo 1-013 ⚪
Posh Pear 1-014 ⚪

::::::::::SEASON 2::::::::::
****** FRUIT & VEG ******

Chloe Flower 2-001 ⚫
Sour Lemon 2-002 ⚫
Juicy Orange 2-003 ⚪
Corny Cob 2-004 ⚫

Garlic Rose 2-005 ⚪
Boo-Hoo Onion 2-006 ⚪
Dippy Avocado 2-007 ⚪
Silly Chilli 2-008 ⚪

Chloe Flower 2-009 ⚪
Sour Lemon 2-010 ⚫
Juicy Orange 2-011 ⚪
Corny Cob 2-012 ⚫

Garlic Rose 2-013 ⚪
Boo-Hoo Onion 2-014 ⚪
Dippy Avocado 2-015 ⚪
Silly Chilli 2-016 ⚪

## SEASON 3
### ★★★★★★ FRUIT & VEG ★★★★★★

Peachy
3-069 ○

Wild
Carrot
3-070 ○

Sweet
Pea
3-071 ○

Pee Wee
Kiwi
3-072 ○

Aspara-
Gus
3-073 ○

Super
Celery
3-074 ●

Asbury
Raspberry
3-075 ○

Cherie
Tomatoe
3-076 ○

Peachy
3-077 ○

Wild
Carrot
3-078 ○

Sweet
Pea
3-079 ○

Pee Wee
Kiwi
3-080 ○

Aspara-
Gus
3-081 ○

Super
Celery
3-082 ●

Asbury
Raspberry
3-083 ○

Cherie
Tomatoe
3-084 ○

## SEASON 4
### ★★★★★★ FRUIT & VEG ★★★★★★

Kris P
Lettuce
4-001 ○

Peely
Potato
4-002 ○

Milly
Mushroom
4-003 ○

Cheeky
Cherries
4-004 ○

April
Apricot
4-005 ●

Kris P
Lettuce
4-006 ○

Peely
Potato
4-007 ○

Milly
Mushroom
4-008 ○

Cheeky
Cherries
4-009 ○

April
Apricot
4-010 ●

## SEASON 1
###### ****** BAKERY ******

| | | | |
|---|---|---|---|
| Bread Head 1-033 | Creamy Bun-Bun 1-034 | D'lish Donut 1-035 | Cheese Kate 1-036 |
| Mini Muffin 1-037 | Flutter Cake 1-038 | Kookie Cookie 1-039 | Bread Head 1-040 |
| Creamy Bun-Bun 1-041 | D'lish Donut 1-042 | Cheese Kate 1-043 | Mini Muffin 1-044 |
| Flutter Cake 1-045 | Kookie Cookie 1-046 | | |

## SEASON 2
###### ****** BAKERY *******

| | | | |
|---|---|---|---|
| Slick Breadstick 2-035 | Mary Muffin 2-036 | Carrie Carrot Cake 2-037 | Mary Meringue 2-038 |
| Pecanna Pie 2-039 | Choco Lava 2-040 | Fifi Fruit Tart 2-041 | Danni Danish 2-042 |
| Cupcake Chic 2-043 | Slick Breadstick 2-044 | Mary Muffin 2-045 | Carrie Carrot Cake 2-046 |
| Mary Meringue 2-047 | Pecanna Pie 2-048 | Choco Lava 2-049 | Fifi Fruit Tart 2-050 |
| Danni Danish 2-051 | Cupcake Chic 2-052 | | |

## SEASON 3
### ******** BAKERY ********

| | | | |
|---|---|---|---|
| Cheese Louise 3-001  ● | Queen of Tarts 3-002  ○ | Patty Cake 3-003  ○ | Lana Banana Bread 3-004  ○ |
| Toastie Bread 3-005  ○ | Candy Cookie 3-006  ○ | Birthday Betty 3-007  ○ | Wendy Wedding Cake 3-008  ● |
| Nilla Slice 3-009  ○ | Cheese Louise 3-010  ● | Queen of Tarts 3-011  ○ | Patty Cake 3-012  ○ |
| Lana Banana Bread 3-013  ○ | Toastie Bread 3-014  ○ | Candy Cookie 3-015  ● | Birthday Betty 3-016 ○ |
| | Wendy Wedding Cake 3-017  ○ | Nilla Slice 3-018  ○ | |

## SEASON 4
### ******** BAKERY ********

| | | | |
|---|---|---|---|
| Bread Crumbs 4-011  ○ | Cookie Nut 4-012  ○ | Cindy Bon 4-013  ○ | Bagel Billy 4-014  ○ |
| Dolly Donut 4-015  ○ | Bread Crumbs 4-016  ○ | Cookie Nut 4-017  ○ | Cindy Bon 4-018  ○ |
| | Bagel Billy 4-019  ○ | Dolly Donut 4-020  ○ | |

## SEASON 1
## ✱✱✱✱✱✱ DAIRY ✱✱✱✱✱✱✱

| Chee Zee 1-065 ○ | Swiss Miss 1-066 ○ | Spilt Milk 1-067 ○ | Ghurty 1-068 ○ |
| Millie Shake 1-069 ● | Flava Ava 1-070 ○ | Dollops 1-071 ○ | Googy 1-072 ○ |
| Chee Zee 1-073 ○ | Swiss Miss 1-074 ○ | Spilt Milk 1-075 ○ | Ghurty 1-076 ○ |
| Millie Shake 1-077 ● | Flava Ava 1-078 ○ | Dollops 1-079 ○ | Googy 1-080 ○ |

## SEASON 1
## ✱✱✱✱✱✱✱ FROZEN ✱✱✱✱✱✱✱✱

| Ice Cream Dream 1-121 ○ | Popsi Cool 1-122 ○ | Yo-Chi 1-123 ○ | Cool Cube 1-124 ○ |
| Pa' Pizza 1-125 ○ | Snow Crush 1-126 ○ | Fishtix 1-127 ○ | Freezy Peazy 1-128 ○ |
| Ice Cream Dream 1-129 ○ | Popsi Cool 1-130 ○ | Yo-Chi 1-131 ○ | Cool Cube 1-132 ○ |
| Pa' Pizza 1-133 ○ | Snow Crush 1-134 ○ | Fishtix 1-135 ○ | Freezy Peazy 1-136 ○ |

# SEASON 2
## *** CLEANING & LAUNDRY ***

| | | | |
|---|---|---|---|
| Dishy Liquid 2-087 | Squeaky Clean 2-088 | Wendy Washer 2-089 | Bree Freshner 2-090 |
| Molly Mops 2-091 | Sweeps 2-092 | Sarah Softner 2-093 | Peta Plunger 2-094 |
| Leafy 2-095 | Dishy Liquid 2-096 | Squeaky Clean 2-097 | Wendy Washer 2-098 |
| Bree Freshner 2-099 | Molly Mops 2-100 | Sweeps 2-101 | Sarah Softner 2-102 |
| | Peta Plunger 2-103 | Leafy 2-104 | |

# SEASON 2
## ******** BABY ********

| | | | |
|---|---|---|---|
| Dribbles 2-121 | Ga Ga Gourmet 2-122 | Dum Mee Mee 2-123 | Baby Swipes 2-124 |
| Sippy Sips 2-125 | Baby Puff 2-126 | Nappy Dee 2-127 | Shampoo Sue 2-128 |
| Dribbles 2-129 | Ga Ga Gourmet 2-130 | Dum Mee Mee 2-131 | Baby Swipes 2-132 |
| Sippy Sips 2-133 | Baby Puff 2-134 | Nappy Dee 2-135 | Shampoo Sue 2-136 |

## SEASON 4
## PETSHOP

Doggy Bowl 4-073
Little Pet Collar 4-074
Dennis Ball 4-075
Pup-E-House 4-076

Kitty Catbed 4-077
Teena Catfood 4-078
Goldie Fish Bowl 4-079
Pup E Brush 4-080

Doggy Bowl 4-081
Little Pet Collar 4-082
Dennis Ball 4-083
Pup-E-House 4-084

Kitty Catbed 4-085
Teena Catfood 4-086
Goldie Fish Bowl 4-087
Pup-E-House 4-088

## SEASON 2
## HOMEWARES

Toasty Pop 2-017
Brenda Blender 2-018
Coffee Drip 2-019
Saucy Pan 2-020

Ma Kettle 2-021
Zappy Microwave 2-022
Lisa Litter 2-023
Lana Lamp 2-024

Sizzles 2-025
Toasty Pop 2-026
Brenda Blender 2-027
Coffee Drip 2-028

Saucy Pan 2-029
Ma Kettle 2-030
Zappy Microwave 2-031
Lisa Litter 2-032

Lana Lamp 2-033
Sizzles 2-034

## SEASON 3
## ****** HOMEWARES *****

**Washa** 3-103 ○

**Vicky Vac** 3-104 ○

**Frost T Fridge** 3-105 ○

**Blow-Anne** 3-106 ○

**Teenie TV** 3-107 ○

**Radio Sue** 3-108 ○

**Chatter** 3-109 ○

**Mobile Mary** 3-110 ○

**Mixie & Maxie** 3-111 ○

**Washa** 3-112 ○

**Vicky Vac** 3-113 ○

**Frost T Fridge** 3-114 ○

**Blow-Anne** 3-115 ○

**Teenie TV** 3-116 ○

**Radio Sue** 3-117 ○

**Chatter** 3-118 ○

**Mobile Mary** 3-119 ○

**Mixie & Maxie** 3-120 ○

## ::::: SEASON 4 :::::
## ****** HOMEWARES *****

**Edgar Eggcup** 4-041 ○

**Comfy Chair** 4-042 ○

**Tammy TV** 4-043 ○

**Gale Scales** 4-044 ○

**Flushes** 4-045 ○

**Edgar Eggcup** 4-046 ○

**Comfy Chair** 4-047 ○

**Tammy TV** 4-048 ○

**Gale Scales** 4-049 ○

**Flushes** 4-050 ○

# SEASON 1
## SWEET TREATS

Bubbles
1-047

Candy Kisses
1-048

Le'Quorice
1-049

Cheeky Chocolate
1-050

Candi Cotton
1-051

Lolli Poppins
1-052

Mandy Candy
1-053

Jelly B
1-054

Miss Twist
1-055

Bubbles
1-056

Candy Kisses
1-057

Le'Quorice
1-058

Cheeky Chocolate
1-059

Candi Cotton
1-060

Lolli Poppins
1-061

Mandy Candy
1-062

Jelly B
1-063

Miss Twist
1-064

# SEASON 2
## SWEET TREATS

Poppy Corn
2-053

Minnie Mintie
2-054

Banana Splitty
2-055

Yummy Gum
2-056

Waffle Sue
2-057

Ice Cream Dream
2-058

Cheery Churro
2-059

Pamela Pancake
2-060

Poppy Corn
2-061

Minnie Mintie
2-062

Banana Splitty
2-063

Yummy Gum
2-064

Waffle Sue
2-065

Ice Cream Dream
2-066

Cheery Churro
2-067

Pamela Pancake
2-068

## SEASON 3
### ★★★★★★ SWEET TREATS ★★★★★★

PopRock
3-051 ⬤ ◯

Cream E
Cookie
3-052 ⬤

Macca
Roon
3-053 ⬤

Chocky
Box
3-054 ⬤

Wanda
Wafer
3-055 ◯

Choc
Kiss
3-056 ⬤

Suzie
Sundae
3-057 ⬤

Candy
Apple
3-058 ◯

Ginger
Fred
3-059 ⬤

PopRock
3-060 ⬤

Cream E
Cookie
3-061 ⬤

Macca
Roon
3-062 ⬤

Chocky
Box
3-063 ⬤

Wanda
Wafer
3-064 ◯

Choc
Kiss
3-065 ⬤

Suzie
Sundae
3-066 ⬤

Candy
Apple
3-067 ◯

Ginger
Fred
3-068 ◯

## SEASON 4
### ★★★★★ SWEET TREATS ★★★★★

Ice Cream
Queen
4-021 ◯

Jiggly
Jelly
4-022 ◯

Pancake
Jake
4-023 ⬤

Berry
Smoothie
4-024 ⬤

Betsy
Buttercup
4-025 ◯

Ice Cream
Queen
4-026 ◯

Jiggly
Jelly
4-027 ◯

Pancake
Jake
4-028 ⬤

Berry
Smoothie
4-029 ⬤

Betsy
Buttercup
4-030 ◯

## SEASON 1
## ★★★★★★ PARTY FOOD ★★★★★

| | | | |
|---|---|---|---|
| Crispy Chip 1-081 ○ | Pretz-elle 1-082 ○ | Wobbles 1-083 ○ | Rainbow Bite 1-084 ○ |
| Wishes 1-085 ● | Frank Furter 1-086 ○ | Little Sipper 1-087 ○ | Fairy Crumbs 1-088 ○ |
| Cheezy B 1-089 ○ | Soda Pops 1-090 ○ | Crispy Chip 1-091 ● | Pretz-elle 1-092 ○ |
| Wobbles 1-093 ○ | Rainbow Bite 1-094 ○ | Wishes 1-095 ● | Frank Furter 1-096 ○ |
| Little Sipper 1-097 ○ | Fairy Crumbs 1-098 ○ | Cheezy B 1-099 ○ | Soda Pops 1-100 ● |

## SEASON 4
## ★★★★★★ PARTY TIME ★★★★★★★

| | | | |
|---|---|---|---|
| Miss Pressy 4-063 ○ | Mary Wishes 4-064 ○ | Marty Party Hat 4-065 ○ | June Balloon 4-066 ○ |
| Party Plate 4-067 ○ | Miss Pressy 4-068 ○ | Mary Wishes 4-069 ○ | Marty Party Hat 4-070 ○ |
| | June Balloon 4-071 ○ | Party Plate 4-072 ○ | |

## SEASON 1
## *** HEALTH & BEAUTY ***

Scrubs
1-101 ○

Lippy Lips
1-102 ○

Curly
1-103 ○

Shampy
1-104 ○

Silky
1-105 ○

Bubble Tubs
1-106 ●

Chap-Elli
1-107 ○

Polly Polish
1-108 ●

Suds
1-109 ○

Toofs
1-110 ●

Scrubs
1-111 ○

Lippy Lips
1-112 ○

Curly
1-113 ○

Shampy
1-114 ○

Silky
1-115 ○

Bubble Tubs
1-116 ●

Chap-Elli
1-117 ●

Polly Polish
1-118 ●

Subs
1-119 ○

Toofs
1-120 ●

## SEASON 3
## ****** STATIONERY ******

Stella Stapler
3-121 ○

Snippy
3-122 ●

Penny Pencil
3-123 ○

Noni Notebook
3-124 ○

Erica Eraser
3-125 ○

Kelly Calculator
3-126 ○

Rita Ruler
3-127 ○

Secret Sally
3-128 ○

Stella Stapler
3-129 ○

Snippy
3-130 ○

Penny Pencil
3-131 ○

Noni Notebook
3-132 ○

Erica Eraser
3-133 ○

Kelly Calculator
3-134 ○

Rita Ruler
3-135 ○

Secret Sally
3-136 ○

## SEASON 2
### SHOES

| Shopkin | Collected | Shopkin | Collected | Shopkin | Collected | Shopkin | Collected |
|---|---|---|---|---|---|---|---|
| Prommy 2-105 | ○ | Sneaky Sue 2-106 | ● | Heels 2-107 | ○ | Sneaky Wedge 2-108 | ○ |
| Betty Boot 2-109 | ● | Wedgy Wendy 2-110 | ○ | Bun Bun Slipper 2-111 | ○ | Cute Boot 2-112 | ● |
| Prommy 2-113 | ○ | Sneaky Sue 2-114 | ● | Heels 2-115 | ○ | Sneaky Wedge 2-116 | ○ |
| Betty Boot 2-117 | ● | Wedgy Wendy 2-118 | ○ | Bun Bun Slipper 2-119 | ○ | Cute Boot 2-120 | ● |

## SEASON 3
### SHOES

| Shopkin | Collected | Shopkin | Collected | Shopkin | Collected | Shopkin | Collected |
|---|---|---|---|---|---|---|---|
| Beverley Heels 3-035 | ○ | Shoes-Anne 3-036 | ○ | Jennifer Rayne 3-037 | ● | Molly Moccasin 3-038 | ● |
| Lizzy Lace-up 3-039 | ● | Sneaky Sally 3-040 | ● | Snug Ugg 3-041 | ○ | Wilma Wedge 3-042 | ○ |
| Beverley Heels 3-043 | ○ | Shoes-Anne 3-044 | ○ | Jennifer Rayne 3-045 | ● | Molly Moccasin 3-046 | ● |
| Lizzy Lace-up 3-047 | ● | Sneaky Sally 3-048 | ● | Snug Ugg 3-049 | ○ | Wilma Wedge 3-050 | ○ |

## SEASON 3
### ******** HATS ********

**Casper Cap 3-019** ○●
**Hattie Hat 3-020** ○
**Flappy Cap 3-021** ○
**Brimmy 3-022** ●

**Toni Topper 3-023** ○●
**Shady 3-024** ○●
**Bonnie Beret 3-025** ○
**Taylor Rayne 3-026** ○

**Casper Cap 3-027** ○●
**Hattie Hat 3-028** ○
**Flappy Cap 3-029** ○
**Brimmy 3-030** ○●

**Toni Topper 3-031** ○●
**Shady 3-032** ○
**Bonnie Beret 3-033** ○
**Taylor Rayne 3-034** ○

## SEASON 4
### ****** ACCESSORIES ******

**Sharon Shoe 4-031** ○
**Handbag Harriet 4-032** ○
**Wooly Hat 4-033** ●
**Jules 4-004** ○

**Sasha Belt 4-035** ○●
**Sharon Shoe 4-036** ○
**Handbag Harriet 4-037** ○
**Wooly Hat 4-038** ○

**Jules 4-039** ○
**Sasha Belt 4-040** ●

## SEASON 3
### *** INTERNATIONAL FOOD ***

| | | | |
|---|---|---|---|
| Suzie Sushi 3-085 | Humpty Dumpling 3-086 | Lammy Lamington 3-087 | Netti Spaghetti 3-088 |
| Croissant d'Or 3-089 | Fiona Fries 3-090 | Sconnie 3-091 | Taco Terrie 3-092 |
| Sausage Sizzle 3-093 | Suzie Sushi 3-094 | Humpty Dumpling 3-095 | Lammy Lamington 3-096 |
| Netti Spaghetti 3-097 | Croissant d'Or 3-098 | Fiona Fries 3-099 | Sconnie 3-100 |
| | Taco Terrie 3-101 | Sausage Sizzle 3-102 | |

## SEASON 4
### ******* GARDEN *********

| | | | |
|---|---|---|---|
| Peta Plant 4-051 | Tiny Tree 4-052 | Will Barrow 4-053 | Prickles 4-054 |
| Pheobe Fork 4-055 | Mintee 4-056 | Peta Plant 4-057 | Tiny Tree 4-058 |
| Will Barrow 4-059 | Prickles 4-060 | Pheobe Fork 4-061 | Mintee 4-062 |

| Jilly Jam 4-089 | Tracey Tomato 4-090 | Shy Pie 4-091 | Jilly Jam 4-092 |
|---|---|---|---|
|  ○ |  ○ |  ○ |  ○ |

| Tracey Tomato 4-093 | Shy Pie 4-094 | Milk Bud 4-095 | Tubby Butter 4-096 |
|---|---|---|---|
|  ○ |  ○ |  ○ |  ○ |

| Hot Choc 4-097 | Milk Bud 4-098 | Tubby Butter 4-099 | Hot Choc 4-100 |
|---|---|---|---|
|  ○ |  ○ |  ○ |  ○ |

| Big Topping 4-101 | Mabel Syrup 4-102 | Ice Cream Cup 4-103 | |
|---|---|---|---|
|  ○ |  ○ |  ○ | |

| Big Topping 4-104 | Mabel Syrup 4-105 | Ice Cream Cup 4-106 | |
|---|---|---|---|
|  ○ |  ○ |  ○ | |

| Bobby Sock 4-107 | Jingle Purse 4-108 | Earring Twins 4-109 | |
|---|---|---|---|
|  ○ |  ○ |  ○ | |

| Bobby Sock 4-110 | Jingle Purse 4-111 | Earring Twins 4-112 | |
|---|---|---|---|
|  ○ |  ○ |  ○ | |

| Eggchic 4-113 | Comfy Cushion 4-114 | Rita Remote 4-115 | Eggchic 4-116 |
|---|---|---|---|
|  ○ |  ○ |  ○ |  ○ |

| Comfy Cushion 4-117 | Rita Remote 4-118 | Drips 4-119 | Burt House 4-120 |
|---|---|---|---|
|  ○ |  ○ |  ○ |  ○ |

| Jade Spade 4-121 | Drips 4-122 | Burt House 4-123 | Jade Spade 4-124 |
|---|---|---|---|
|  ○ |  ○ |  ○ |  ○ |

| Bone-adette 4-125 | Waggy Tag 4-126 | Fish Flake Jake 4-127 | Bone-adette 4-128 |
|---|---|---|---|
|  ○ |  ○ |  ○ |  ○ |

| Waggy Tag 4-129 | Fish Flake Jake 4-130 | Dinky Drink 4-131 | Flicker Candle 4-132 |
|---|---|---|---|
|  ○ |  ○ |  ○ |  ○ |

| Whistle Wilma 4-133 | Dinky Drink 4-134 | Flicker Candle 4-135 | Whistle Wilma 4-136 |
|---|---|---|---|
|  ○ |  ○ |  ○ |  ○ |

## SEASON 1
## ★★★★★ LIMITED EDITION ★★★★★

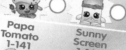

Cupcake Queen 1-137 ○
Buttercup 1-138 ○
Tin 'a' Tuna 1-139 ○
Twinky Winks 1-140 ○

Papa Tomato 1-141 ○
Sunny Screen 1-142 ○

## SEASON 2

## ★★★★★ LIMITED EDITION ★★★★★

Marsha Mellow 2-137 ○
Rub-a-Glove 2-138 ○
Lenny Lime 2-139 ○
Lee Tea 2-140 ○

Donna Donut 2-141 ○
Angie Ankle Boot 2-142 ○

## SEASON 3
## ★★★★★ LIMITED EDITION ★★★★★

Ruby Earring 3-137 ○
Chelsea Charm 3-138 ○
Ring-A-Rosie 3-139 ○
Ticky Tock 3-140 ○

Brenda Brooch 3-141 ○
Roxy Ring 3-142 ○

## SEASON 4
## ★★★★★ LIMITED EDITION ★★★★★

Frenchy Perfume 4-137 ○
Pretty Puff 4-138 ○
Sparkly Spritz 4-139 ○
Pretty Bow Kay 4-140 ○

Gemma Bottle 4-141 ○
Sally Scent 4-142 ○